# NORA THE NONAPUS

Written and Illustrated by:

ZOE GAN  SUSAN CAVENDER

VAISHNAVI KRISHNAN  ALISON SMITH

Copyright © 2004 by Scholastic Inc
Scholastic and associated logos are trademarks and/or registered trademarks of Scholastic Inc
ISBN 0-439-71898-8

12 11 10 9 8 7 6 5 4 3 2 1

Book Design by Bill Henderson
Printed and bound in the U.S.A.

First Printing, July 2004

The sea is home to many octopuses and even a few bullypuses, but there is only one nonapus, and her name is Nora. Nora was like any other octopus except she had one extra tentacle. Because she was different, she was afraid of being teased. So she always tried to keep her ninth tentacle hidden.

**W**hen swimming to school, she hid her tentacle in her backpack. At school, Nora tucked it into her desk. If there was no place to hide the tentacle, she managed to pull it up into her body even though her muscles felt a little cramped.

**N**ora didn't have any friends.  Her classmates thought she was nice, but a little strange.  She sat by herself during class and she always ate lunch alone.

Everyday at lunch her classmates would say, "Come sit with us, Nora," and everyday Nora would say, "No, not today." While the little octopuses played and laughed outside during recess, Nora sat inside the classroom feeling miserable.

Everyday they would say, "C'mon Nora, come out and play," and everyday Nora would say, "No, not today."  She wanted to go outside and play but she was afraid that everyone would notice her extra tentacle and make fun of her.

One day the door to the classroom burst open and a new kid walked in. His name was Boyd. He was big and strong and towered over the other octopuses. As Boyd stomped to take his seat, the floor of the classroom shook and the windows rattled. He scowled at everyone and stared with a mean glint in his eyes. He had a green body with powerful tentacles that looked threatening. The kids feared that Boyd might be a bullypus, but, then again, they did not want to judge him by his looks.

However, at recess, their worst fears came true. Boyd juggled Otto, Ollie and Allan, as though they were little balls, and gave them headaches for the rest of the day. At lunch, he snatched poor Coral's mackerel sandwich and gobbled it down. No one dared to stop him. Nora tried harder than ever to hide her ninth tentacle from everyone, especially Boyd, the bullypus. Boyd continued to bully the kids everyday. The kids were too scared of Boyd to report him to their teacher. So their teacher, Mrs. Tentaloupe, never found out about Boyd's bad behavior.

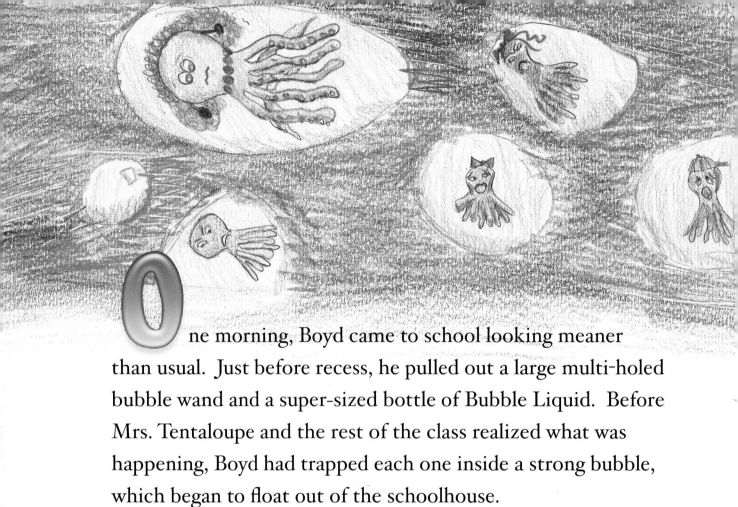

One morning, Boyd came to school looking meaner than usual. Just before recess, he pulled out a large multi-holed bubble wand and a super-sized bottle of Bubble Liquid. Before Mrs. Tentaloupe and the rest of the class realized what was happening, Boyd had trapped each one inside a strong bubble, which began to float out of the schoolhouse.

The terrified octopuses looked through the clear walls of their prisons and saw that they were drifting toward a huge mountain. Trying to break free, they pushed against the walls of the bubbles. But the bubbles would not pop. Boyd just watched and laughed. Floating closer toward the mountain, Nora and the others realized that it was actually a gigantic volcano, and Boyd was gleefully leading them inside.

Hardened black lava and slimy green algae coated the sides of the rumbling volcano, and seaweed thickly covered its base.  Boyd made his way to a passage hidden in the seaweed and pushed his struggling prisoners inside.  Nora shivered with fear and wondered whether the volcano would explode.

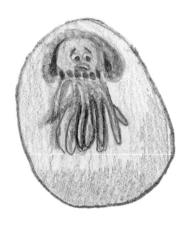

The short passage led to a door, which opened into a huge dark cave. Dozens of ropes made of seaweed hung from its high ceiling. Boyd popped the bubbles one by one and tied the trembling octopuses to the ropes.

Watching them struggle against the ropes, Boyd knew that the little octopuses were too weak to wriggle out of the tight knots. Cackling loudly, he left the room not even bothering to lock the door behind him.

The little octopuses wailed and sobbed, wondering what Boyd was going to do to them.  Mrs. Tentaloupe tried to comfort them as best as she could while Nora quietly looked around.  She saw that all the octopuses were strung up by their eight tentacles, unable to free themselves.

Then she remembered that she had nine!  In the midst of all the confusion, she had forgotten about her ninth tentacle, which she had managed to keep tucked inside her body the entire time.

Trying not to attract the attention of her classmates, Nora slowly slipped her ninth tentacle out from inside her body and reached toward the knot that bound her. She was tense as her small, weak tentacle poked and tugged at the thick knot. The task seemed impossible, but Nora knew that the safety of her entire class depended on her.

As she slowly loosened the knot and freed herself, Nora noticed that Mrs. Tentaloupe and the others were staring at her ninth tentacle in disbelief. Nora ignored their stares as she hurried to untie her teacher.

Ollie, the littlest octopus squeaked, "Untie me first, please." This was followed by a chorus of other voices shouting, "No, please, me first," and "How about me?"

"Shush," warned Mrs. Tentaloupe, "Boyd might be listening."

While untying her friends, Nora noticed that Boyd had left the key in the passage door. She also noticed a small hole in a corner of the ceiling through which a sliver of light was peeking. An idea flashed through Nora's mind. She gathered all her friends around her and explained to them her plan to trap Boyd and teach him a lesson.

One by one, the octopuses swam up toward the hole in the ceiling. Nora quietly locked the door and followed her friends out of the volcano. They then hid among the seaweed and waited for Boyd's return.

A few minutes later they saw Boyd swim up to the door and try to open it. He looked puzzled when the door did not open. He then tried to rattle it, but it wouldn't move. Boyd began to get annoyed and started to bang on the door trying to break it down, but the door was strong. Then he tried to pull the door off its hinges.

His muscles bulged, and his face turned red as he tried to tear the door out, but the sturdy door just stayed shut. Boyd stopped, thought for a minute, and began to head toward the hole on the top.

**N**ora and the others exchanged smiles of delight as they watched Boyd try to squeeze his big body into the tiny hole. Boyd managed with great difficulty to fit his tentacles trough the hole and continued to squeeze himself down the tight space. The little octopuses began to get nervous as they watched Boyd inch his way down. "He might make it down the hole and into the cave," they thought in dismay. Then, all of a sudden Boyd stopped moving. The octopuses watched as Boyd's face turned red with fury. He tried to wriggle himself out of the hole and back upward. His face contorted with the effort, but he did not budge an inch. Boyd was stuck!

The octopuses jumped up and down cheering excitedly. Boyd was a sight to see. With his tentacles inside the hole and his head on top, he looked like a big red golf ball sitting on top of a giant tee. Nora's plan had worked. Her friends thought she was awesome and praised her smartness and courage.

When the cheering died down, Allan asked, "Why do you have nine tentacles, Nora?" Someone else added, "That's so cool. Why didn't you tell us?" Nora finally understood that it was okay to be different and felt foolish for hiding herself from her friends for so long.

re you wondering what happened to Boyd? After much pleading and tentacle-squirming, he made a deal with Mrs. Tentaloupe, Nora and the rest of the group. If they helped pull him out of the hole, he promised he would never bully anybody again.

He also agreed to stay back for detention every day for the rest of the year. And for two hours every day after school, Boyd learned good manners, proper behavior and kindness toward all fellow creatures.

TENTION BOARD FOR NAUGHTY OCTOPUSES
will not juggle my classmates.
will juggle balls instead.
will not steal food.
will bring my own food
will not try to bully others.
will not try to bully others.
will not try to bully others.
will try to be polite to others.
I will try to be polite to o
INSTRUCTIONS for BOYD:
Room 104
STUDE
1. BOY
2.
3.
4.
5.
6.

For Mrs. Ghada Ramadan, our fifth grade teacher
With gratitude, respect and love

With special thanks to our parents
for their support and encouragement

Kids Are Authors ®
Books written by children for children

The Kids Are Authors ® Competition was established in 1986 to encourage children to read and to become involved in the creative process of writing. Since then, thousands of children have written and illustrated books as participants in the Kids Are Authors ® Competition. The winning books in the annual competition are published by Scholastic Inc. and are distributed by Scholastic Book Fairs throughout the United States.

For more information:
Kids Are Authors®
1080 Greenwood Blvd.
Lake Mary, FL 32746

Or visit our web site at:
www.scholastic.com/kidsareauthors